For Janno and Danielle-
LOVE!

At school, Shira learned
all about Rosh Hashanah.
She learned that
ROSH רֹאשׁ means head in Hebrew,
and SHANAH שָׁנָה is year- the
beginning of a new year.
She also learned about the
Shofar שׁוֹפָר and its sounds, greeting
cards for a happy new year and
the foods we celebrate with: apples
and honey for a sweet year –

שֶׁתִּתְחַדֵּשׁ עָלֵינוּ שָׁנָה טוֹבָה וּמְתוּקָה

round challah for the circle of life,
fish with its head for being leaders-

שֶׁנִּהְיֶה לְרֹאשׁ וְלֹא לְזָנָב

(head and not a tail) . . .

2

SHANAH TOVAH!

3

. . . and the RIMON רִמּוֹן fruit for lots of MITZVOT (commandments) מִצְווֹת in the New Year

שֶׁיִּרְבּוּ זְכֻיּוֹתֵינוּ כְּרִמּוֹן

During class, her teacher presented the RIMON, and explained that we eat it because we want to fulfill as many MITZVOT מִצְווֹת in the new year as there are seeds in the RIMON.

4

6

Because it was a new fruit for the students, the teacher added, "When we eat a new fruit for the first time, we recite the blessing: "SHEHECHEYANU" שֶׁהֶחֱיָנוּ

"בָּרוּךְ אַתָּה ה', אֱלוֹהֵינוּ מֶלֶךְ הָעוֹלָם, שֶׁהֶחֱיָנוּ וְקִיְּמָנוּ וְהִגִּיעָנוּ לַזְּמַן הַזֶּה"

The teacher cut the fruit and Shira said, "Wow, this is so cool!" and when she tasted it for the first time ever, she loved it.

רִמּוֹן

8

At home, Shira couldn't wait to tell her parents about what she had learned about Rosh Hashanah and asked, "Please, take me to the store to get a RIMON; I just love it and we should have it on our holiday table this year."

"Okay, I was going to the store anyway. Come with me," answered her mother.

At the supermarket, Shira politely asked the produce attendant, "Where can I find a RIMON, please?"

The attendant replied, "Sorry, little girl, we don't have such fruit."

11

Shira was so
disappointed and sad.
Her mother said,
"Don't be sad, honey.
There is a fruit stand
outside this store; let's
check there."

At the fruit stand Shira
said to the merchant,
"I am looking for a RIMON.
Do you have some?"

The merchant replied,
"I have been selling fruit
for a long time and have
never heard of a RIMON."

15

Shira's face was long; she looked at the floor and felt like she was about to cry. Her mother wanted to help Shira and said, "We can go to the store across the street; perhaps they have a RIMON."

17

As they entered the store, Shira looked right in front of her, opened her mouth, and froze; she saw a large bin, packed full of the RIMON fruit. She ran to it, pointed to the bin, jumped up and down and shouted, "Mom, look, RIMON, we found it! We are going to have a new year full of MITZVOT מִצְווֹת, we are!"

19

She was so excited and happy. Her mother kneeled next to her and explained with a smile, "Shira, honey, this fruit is called RIMON in Hebrew, but in English it is called a pomegranate."

Shira took a plastic bag and filled it with the delicious, red fruit and said to her mom, laughing, "For me, this fruit will always be a RIMON. . ."

Rosh Hashanah dinner
was complete with all
the traditional foods, and
especially the RIMON. . .

רִמוֹן

שָׁנָה טוֹבָה!

23

The story behind the story:

The author, Galia Sabbag, is a veteran Hebrew teacher of over fifteen years at The Davis Academy, a Reform Jewish Day School in Atlanta Ga. During her years of teaching, she has come across profound examples of how school affects families and their home life and how children grow in Jewish knowledge and spirituality. By witnessing these "aha" moments and/or by listening to parents' and grandparents' anecdotes, a series of stories emerged, and became lovable "Shira." She is the culminating sum of all Mrs. Sabbag's students throughout the years all put together. Most of the stories in the series are real ones that actually happened to real students, interwoven with the author's creativity.

As a Hebrew teacher, Mrs. Sabbag has sprinkled Hebrew words, songs, greetings and blessings throughout every story.
These stories will appeal to children in Jewish preschools, Sunday school or Jewish day schools and of course, in every Jewish home.

Coming soon in the series:
Shira at the Temple - a Yom Kippur story
Shira in the Sukkah - a Sukkot story
Shira and the Torah - a Simchat Torah story
Miracle for Shira- a Chanukah story
and many, many more....

If you enjoyed "RIMON for Shira," you will love another story in the Shira series: "Shabbat in the Playroom."
The eBook is available on Amazon Kindle and on Barnes and Noble Nook. Printed copies are available through the website.

Please check out the websit:
www.shirasseries.com,
twitter: @shirasSeries,
or the facebook page: www.Facebook.com/Shira.series

Made in the USA
Columbia, SC
19 September 2019